On the High Wire

Philippe Petit

On the High Wire

*translated from the French
with an introduction
by Paul Auster*

A NEW DIRECTIONS PAPERBOOK

On the High Wire was originally published by Random House, Inc.
The introduction was originally published in *The Art of Hunger*, Sun
and Moon Press

First published as New Directions Paperbook 1450 in 2019
Manufactured in the United States of America
New Directions Books are printed on acid-free paper
Design by Erik Rieselbach

Library of Congress Cataloging-in-Publication Data
Names: Petit, Philippe, 1949– author. | Auster, Paul, 1947– translator,
author of introduction.
Title: On the high wire / Philippe Petit ; translated, with an intro-
duction, by Paul Auster.
Other titles: Traité du funambulisme. English
Description: New York : New Directions Books, 2019.
Identifiers: LCCN 2019007707 | ISBN 9780811228640 (alk. paper)
Subjects: LCSH: Tightrope walking.
Classification: LCC GV553 .P4713 2019 | DDC 796.46—dc23
LC record available at https://lccn.loc.gov/201900770

10 9 8 7 6 5 4 3 2 1

New Directions Books are published for James Laughlin
by New Directions Publishing Corporation
80 Eighth Avenue, New York 10011

For Francis Brunn, legendary juggler with a graceful disregard for gravity.

To James Signorelli, moving mountains across the seas by keeping an eye on the right wind . . .
You taught me how to secure a bowline with one hand.
And
to Cordia-Gypsy, who just learned to place one foot in front of the other, wishing her the most celestial path.

Contents

INTRODUCTION

I first crossed paths with Philippe Petit in 1971. I
was in Paris, walking down the Boulevard Montparnasse, when I came upon a large circle of people
standing silently on the sidewalk. It seemed clear
that something was happening inside that circle,
and I wanted to know what it was. I elbowed my
way past several onlookers, stood on my toes, and
caught sight of a smallish young man in the center.
Everything he wore was black: his shoes, his pants,
his shirt, even the battered silk top hat he wore on
his head. The hair jutting out from under the hat
was a light red-blond, and the face below it was so
pale, so devoid of color, that at first I thought he
was in whiteface.

The young man juggled, rode a unicycle, performed little magic tricks. He juggled rubber balls,
wooden clubs, and burning torches, both standing on the ground and sitting on his one-wheeler,

moving from one thing to the next without interruption. To my surprise, he did all this in silence. A chalk circle had been drawn on the sidewalk, and scrupulously keeping any of the spectators from entering that space — with a persuasive mime's gesture — he went through his performance with such ferocity and intelligence that it was impossible to stop watching.

Unlike other street performers, he did not play to the crowd. Rather, it was as if he had allowed the audience to share in the workings of his thoughts, had made us privy to some deep, inarticulate obsession within him. Yet there was nothing overtly personal about what he did. Everything was revealed metaphorically, as if at one remove, through the medium of the performance. His juggling was precise and self-involved, like some conversation he was holding with himself. He elaborated the most complex combinations, intricate mathematical patterns, arabesques of nonsensical beauty, while at the same time keeping his gestures as simple as possible. Through it all, he managed to radiate a hypnotic charm, oscillating somewhere between demon and clown. No one said a word. It was as though his silence were a command for others to be silent as well. The crowd watched, and after the performance was over, everyone put money in the hat. I realized that I had never seen anything like it before.

The next time I crossed paths with Philippe Petit was several weeks later. It was late at night—perhaps one or two in the morning—and I was walking along a quai of the Seine not far from Notre Dame. Suddenly, across the street, I spotted several young people moving quickly through the darkness. They were carrying ropes, cables, tools, and heavy satchels. Curious as ever, I kept pace with them from my side of the street and recognized one of them as the juggler from the Boulevard Montparnasse. I knew immediately that something was going to happen. But I could not begin to imagine what it was.

The next day, on the front page of the *International Herald Tribune*, I got my answer. A young man had strung a wire between the towers of Notre Dame Cathedral and walked and juggled and danced on it for three hours, astounding the crowds of people below. No one knew how he had rigged up his wire nor how he had managed to elude the attention of the authorities. Upon returning to the ground, he had been arrested, charged with disturbing the peace and sundry other offenses. It was in this article that I first learned his name: Philippe Petit. There was not the slightest doubt in my mind that he and the juggler were the same person.

This Notre Dame escapade made a deep impression on me, and I continued to think about it over the years that followed. Each time I walked past Notre Dame, I kept seeing the photograph that had been published in the newspaper: an almost invisible wire stretched between the enormous towers of the cathedral, and there, right in the middle, as if suspended magically in space, the tiniest of human figures, a dot of life against the sky. It was impossible for me not to add this remembered image to the actual cathedral before my eyes, as if this old monument of Paris, built so long ago to the glory of God, had been transformed into something else. But what? It was difficult for me to say. Into something more human, perhaps. As though its stones now bore the mark of a man. And yet, there was no real mark. I had made the mark with my own mind, and it existed only in memory. And yet, the evidence was irrefutable: my perception of Paris had changed. I no longer saw it in the same way.

It is, of course, an extraordinary thing to walk

on a wire so high off the ground. To see someone do this triggers an almost palpable excitement in us. In fact, given the necessary courage and skill, there are probably few people who would not want to do it themselves. And yet, the art of high-wire walking has never been taken seriously. Because wire walking generally takes place in the circus, it is automatically assigned marginal status. The circus, after all, is for children, and what do children know about art? We grownups have more important things to think about. There is the art of music, the art of painting, the art of sculpture, the art of poetry, the art of prose, the art of theater, the art of dancing, the art of cooking, the art of living. But the art of high-wire walking? The very term seems laughable. If people stop to think about the high wire at all, they usually categorize it as some minor form of athletics.

There is, too, the problem of showmanship. I mean the crazy stunts, the vulgar self-promotion, the hunger for publicity that is everywhere around us. We live in an age when people seem willing to do anything for a little attention. And the public accepts this, granting notoriety or fame to anyone brave enough or foolish enough to make the effort.

As a general rule, the more dangerous the stunt, the greater the recognition. Cross the ocean in a bathtub, vault forty burning barrels on a motorcycle, dive into the East River from the top of the Brooklyn Bridge, and you are sure to get your name in the newspapers, maybe even an interview on a talk show. The idiocy of these antics is obvious. I'd much rather spend my time watching my son ride his bicycle, training wheels and all.

Danger, however, is an inherent part of high-wire walking. When a man walks on a wire two inches off the ground, we do not respond in the same way as when he walks on a wire two hundred feet off the ground. But danger is only half of it. Unlike the stuntman, whose performance is calculated to emphasize every hair-raising risk, to keep his audience panting with dread and an almost sadistic anticipation of disaster, the good high-wire walker strives to make his audience forget the dangers, to lure it away from thoughts of death by the beauty of what he does on the wire itself. Working under the greatest possible constraints, on a stage no more than an inch wide, the high-wire walker's job is to create a sensation of limitless freedom. Juggler, dancer, acrobat, he performs in the sky what other men are content to perform on the ground. The desire is at once far-fetched and perfectly natural, and the appeal of it, finally, is its utter uselessness. No art, it seems to me, so clearly emphasizes the deep aesthetic impulse inside us all. Each time we see a man walk on the wire, a part of us is up there with him. Unlike performances in the other arts, the experience of the high wire is direct, unmediated, simple, and it requires no explanation whatsoever. The art is the thing itself, a life in its most naked delineation. And if there is beauty in this, it is because of the beauty we feel inside ourselves.

There was another element of the Notre Dame spectacle that moved me: the fact that it was clandestine. With the thoroughness of a bank robber preparing a heist, Philippe had gone about his business in silence. No press conferences, no publicity, no posters. The purity of it was impressive. For what could he possibly hope to gain? If the wire had snapped, if the installation had been faulty, he would have died. On the other hand, what did success bring? Certainly he did not earn any money from the venture. He did not even try to capitalize on his brief moment of glory. When all was said and done, the only tangible result was a short stay in a Paris jail.

Why did he do it, then? For no other reason, I believe, than to dazzle the world with what he could do. Having seen his stark and haunting juggling performance on the street, I sensed intuitively that his motives were not those of other men—not even those of other artists. With an ambition and an arrogance fit to the measure of the sky, and placing on himself the most stringent internal demands, he wanted, simply, to do what he was capable of doing.

After living in France for four years, I returned to New York in July 1974. For a long time I had heard nothing about Philippe Petit, but the memory of what had happened in Paris was still fresh, a permanent part of my inner mythology. Then, just one month after my return, Philippe was in the news again—this time in New York, with his now-famous walk between the towers of the World Trade Center. It was good to know that Philippe was still dreaming his dreams, and it made me feel that I had chosen the right moment to come home. New York is a more generous city than Paris, and the people here responded enthusiastically to what he had done. As with the aftermath of the Notre Dame adventure, however, Philippe kept faith with his vision. He did not try to cash in on his new celebrity; he managed to resist the honky-tonk temptations America is all too willing to offer. No books were published, no films were made, no entrepreneur took hold of him for packaging. The fact that the World Trade Center did not make him rich was almost as remarkable as the event itself. But the proof of this was there for all New Yorkers to see: Philippe continued to make his living by juggling in the streets.

The streets were his first theater, and he still takes his performances there as seriously as his work on the wire. It all started very early for him. Born into a middle-class French family in 1949, he taught himself magic at the age of six, juggling at the age of twelve, and high-wire walking a few years later. In the meantime, while immersing himself in such varied activities as horseback riding, rock climbing, art, and carpentry, he managed to get himself expelled from nine schools. At sixteen, he began a period of incessant travels all over the world, performing as a street juggler in Western Europe, Russia, India, Australia, and the United States. "I learned to live by my wits," he has said of those years. "I offered juggling shows everywhere, for everyone — traveling around like a troubadour with my old leather sack. I learned to escape the police on my unicycle. I got hungry like a wolf; I learned how to control my life."

But it is on the high wire that Philippe has concentrated his most important ambitions. In 1973, just two years after the Notre Dame walk, he did another renegade performance in Sydney, Australia: stretching his wire between the northern pylons of the Harbour Bridge, the largest steel arch bridge in the world. Following the World Trade Center walk in 1974, he crossed the Great Falls of Paterson, New Jersey, appeared on television for a walk between the spires of the Cathedral in Laon, France, and also crossed the Superdome in New Orleans before 80,000 people. This last performance took place just nine months after a forty-foot fall from an inclined wire, from which he suffered several broken ribs, a collapsed lung, a shattered hip, and a smashed pancreas.

Philippe has also worked in the circus. For one year he was a featured attraction with Ringling Bros. and Barnum & Bailey, and from time to time he has served as a guest performer with the Big Apple Circus in New York. But the traditional circus has never been the right place for Philippe's talents, and he knows it. He is too solitary and unconventional an artist to fit comfortably into the strictures of the commercial big top. Far more important to him are his plans for the future: to walk across Niagara Falls; to walk from the top of the Sydney Opera House to the top of the Harbour Bridge — an inclined walk of more than half a mile. As he himself explains it: "To talk about records or risks is to miss the point. All my life I have looked for the most amazing places to cross — mountains, waterfalls, buildings. And if the most beautiful walks also happen to be the longest or most dangerous — that's fine. But I didn't look for that in the first place. What interests me is the performance, the show, the beautiful gesture."

When I finally met Philippe in 1980, I realized that all my feelings about him had been correct. This was not a daredevil or a stuntman, but a singular artist who could talk about his work with intelligence and humor. As he said to me that day, he didn't want people to think of him as just another "dumb acrobat." He talked about some of the things he had written — poems, narratives of his Notre Dame and World Trade Center adventures, film scripts, a small book on high-wire walking —

and I said that I would be interested in seeing them. Several days later, I received a bulky package of manuscripts in the mail. A covering note explained that these writings had been rejected by eighteen different publishers in France and America. I did not consider this to be an obstacle. I told Philippe that I would do all I could to find him a publisher and also promised to serve as translator if necessary. Given the pleasure I had received from his performances on the street and wire, it seemed the least I could do.

On the High Wire is in my opinion a remarkable book. Not only is it the first study of high-wire walking ever written, but it is also a personal testament. One learns from it both the art and science of wire walking, the lyricism and the technical demands of the craft. At the same time, it should not be misconstrued as a "how to" book or an instruction manual. High-wire walking cannot really be taught: it is something you learn by yourself. And certainly a book would be the last place to turn if you were truly serious about doing it.

The book, then, is a kind of parable, a spiritual journey in the form of a treatise. Through it all, one feels the presence of Philippe himself: it is his wire, his art, his personality that inform the entire discourse. No one else, finally, has a place in it. This is perhaps the most important lesson to be learned from the book: the high wire is an art of solitude, a way of coming to grips with one's life in the darkest, most secret corner of the self. When read carefully, the book is transformed into the story of a quest, an exemplary tale of one man's search for perfection. As such, it has more to do with the inner life than the high wire. It seems to me that anyone who has ever tried to do something well, anyone who has ever made personal sacrifices for an art or an idea, will have no trouble understanding what it is about.

Until two months ago, I had never seen Philippe perform on the high wire outdoors. A performance or two in the circus, and of course films and photographs of his exploits, but no outdoor walk in the flesh. I finally got my chance during the recent inauguration ceremony at the Cathedral of Saint John the Divine in New York. After a hiatus of several decades, construction was about to begin again on the cathedral's tower. As a kind of homage to the wire walkers of the Middle Ages — the *joglar* from the period of the great French cathedrals — Philippe had conceived the idea of stretching steel cable from the top of a tall apartment building on Amsterdam Avenue to the top of the Cathedral across the street—an inclined walk of several hundred yards. He would go from one end to the other and then present the Bishop of New York with a silver trowel, which would be used to lay the symbolic first stone of the tower.

The preliminary speeches lasted a long time. One after the other, dignitaries got up and spoke about the Cathedral and the historic moment that was about to take place. Clergymen, city officials, former Secretary of State Cyrus Vance—all of them made speeches. A large crowd had gathered in the street, mostly schoolchildren and neighborhood people, and it was clear that the majority of them had come to see Philippe. As the speeches droned on, there was a good deal of talking and restlessness in the crowd. The late September weather was threatening: a raw, pale gray sky; the wind beginning to rise; rain clouds gathering in the distance. Everyone was impatient. If the speeches went on any longer, perhaps the walk would have to be canceled.

Fortunately, the weather held, and at last Philippe's turn came. The area below the cable had to be cleared of people, which meant that those who a moment before had held center stage were now pushed to the side with the rest of us. The democracy of it pleased me. By chance, I found myself standing shoulder to shoulder with Cyrus Vance on the steps of the Cathedral. I, in my beat-up leather jacket, and he in his impeccable blue suit. But that didn't seem to matter. He was just as excited as I was. I realized later that at any other time I might have been tongue-tied to be standing next to such an important person. But none of that even occurred to me then. We talked about the high wire and the dangers Phillipe would have to face. He seemed to be genuinely in awe of the whole thing and kept looking up at the wire — as I did, as did the hundreds of children around us. It was then that I understood the most important aspect of the high wire: it reduces us all to our common humanity. A secretary of state, a poet, a child: we became equal in one another's eyes, and therefore a part of one another.

A brass band played a Renaissance fanfare from some invisible place behind the Cathedral façade, and Philippe emerged from the roof of the building on the other side of the street. He was dressed in a white satin medieval costume, the silver trowel hanging from a sash at his side. He saluted the crowd with a graceful, bravura gesture, took hold of his balancing pole firmly in his two hands, and began his slow ascent along the wire. Step by step, I felt myself walking up there with him, and gradually those heights seemed to become habitable, human, filled with happiness. He slid down to one knee and acknowledged the crowd again; he balanced on one foot; he moved deliberately and majestically, exuding confidence. Then, suddenly, he came to a spot on the wire far enough away from his starting-point that my eyes lost contact with all surrounding references: the apartment building, the street, the other people. He was almost directly overhead now, and as I leaned backward to take in the spectacle, I could see no more than the wire, Philippe, and the sky. There was nothing else. A white body against a nearly white sky, as if free. The purity of that image burned itself into my mind and is still there today, wholly present.

From beginning to end, not once did I think he might fall. Risk, fear of death, catastrophe: these were not part of the performance. Philippe had assumed full responsibility for what he was doing, and I sensed that nothing could possibly shake that resolve. High-wire walking is not an art of death but an art of life — and life lived to the very extreme of life. Which is to say, life that does not hide from death but stares it directly in the face. Each time he sets foot on the wire, Philippe takes hold of that life and lives it in all its exhilarating immediacy, in all its heroic, high-stepping joy.

May he live to be a hundred.

PAUL AUSTER, 1982

On the High Wire

This is the journey to be made:
Rise up as your wire merges with the map of the sky.

Definitions

Whoever walks, dances, or performs
on a rope raised several yards from the ground
is not a high-wire walker.
His wire can be tight or slack; it can bounce
or be completely loose. He works with or without
a balancing pole.
He is called the ropedancer.

Whoever uses a thin wire of brass or steel
in the same way
becomes a low-wire artist.

There remains the one whose performance is a
game of chance.
The one who is proud of his fear.
He dares to stretch his cable over precipices,
he attacks bell towers,
he separates mountains and brings them together.

His steel cable, his rope, must be extremely tight.
He uses a balancing pole for great crossings.
He is the *Voleur* of the Middle Ages,
the *Ascensioniste* of Blondin's time,
the *Funambule*.

In English we call him the High-Wire Walker.

Warning

No, the high wire is not what you think it is.
It is not a realm of lightness, space, and smiles.
It is a job.
Grim, tough, deceptive.

And whoever does not want to struggle
against failure, against danger,
whoever is not prepared to give everything
to feel that he is alive,
does not need to be a high-wire walker.
Nor could he ever become one.

As for this book—
the study of the high wire is not rigorous,
it is useless.

Setting up the wire

There are ropes made of natural fibers, artificial fibers, and metal fibers. When they are stretched, twisted, rolled, compressed, or submitted to rapidly changing temperatures, these fibers create a wire.

The wires are put together to form a strand. Several strands braided, twisted, or sheathed together become a rope. A rope often has in its center a strand of some other material. This is usually called the core, the "soul."

Wires, strands, and soul are assembled according to methods whose laws are as rigorous as they are varied.

The number of ropes, therefore, is infinite.

Whoever intends to master the art of walking on them must take on the task of seeking them out. Of comparing them. Of keeping those whose properties correspond to his aspirations. Of learning how to knot them. Of knowing how to tighten them.

Acquiring this knowledge is the work of a lifetime.

For now, take a metal rope of clear steel, composed of six, seven, or eight strands, with a diameter of between twelve and twenty-six millimeters.

With a soul of hemp.

Today, one no longer finds high-wire walkers who use thick ropes of Italian hemp. For reasons of convenience, the steel cable has replaced the rope.

This cable must be free of all traces of grease.

Each steel cable is lubricated when it is manufactured. The first operation, therefore, is to remove this grease. The best method is to stretch out the cable in the corner of a garden and to leave it there for several years. At the end of that time, you will hunt through the tall grass to retake possession of the "old" cable. To make it new again, wash it in gasoline and rub it with emery until it is clean and gray. It is a good idea to leave a considerable length of cable exposed in this fashion, perhaps five hundred meters. Walk-lengths can then be cut off when needed.

If you are not in a position to age a new cable in this manner, an alternative is to repeat the cleaning process as many times as necessary—to wipe each strand, one after the other, and to go through the operation again and again until the wire is absolutely dry. This method is not entirely satisfactory, however, since the grease that lurks in the soul can sometimes spill forth abundantly when a tightly stretched cable has been exposed to the sun for a prolonged period.

A rusted cable can be made excellent once it has been brushed and wiped.

A cable must be in good condition. Without kinks or meat hooks. Kinks are the traces left by an old loop or hook: the cable has been twisted, and when it is stretched out, a barely perceptible bump remains that even the greatest tension cannot eliminate. Meat hooks are the wires of a broken strand; they bristle up like splinters. To make sure that the cable is not concealing any meat hooks, run a cloth along the entire length of the wire in both directions.

When setting up for the first time, use a simple wire ten meters long, stretched out two and a half meters off the ground between two small poles— two X's of wood or metal—or, even more simply, between two trees. Preferably, trees with character. Attach one end with wire clamps; on the other end attach a tightening device (a large turnbuckle or a level hoist) to a sling. At the tip of the cable make a spliced eye with a thimble inside it. Draw the eye toward the hoist hook with the help of a pulley block. Fasten to the hoist and tighten. Be careful to wrap the tree trunks with large jute cloths so they are not hurt by the wire.

The first steps

The first steps, of course, can be made on a small wire stretched out just two inches from the ground. But then, you could just as easily close this book and become a weekend wire walker.

Don't look for a ladder; leap up onto the wire. Slippers and balancing pole are for later.

Right away, balance yourself on one foot, facing the tree. Quick. Try to hold on as long as possible before grabbing the tree again.

Do not jump. Do not walk. The leg is fixed. The foot is poised along the wire.

Your arms will wave about wildly. Pay no attention to them. Look for balance. Enough! Change feet. Just a little try. Change again. In this way you will find your better foot, the one that will later become your "balancing foot." Then you will stop these stupid gymnastics, turn around, and lean your back against the tree.

High-wire walking is not a solution to the problem of balance.

Look intensely at what stretches out before you. You are facing the cable.

That's it.

Everything changes now that the wire is there.

Fix your eyes on the target—the end—and try a crossing. Don't look for the bark behind you, but jump down the moment you lose your balance. In this way, the crossing will be a series of balancings: on one foot, on the other foot, again, and again, and again.

You must not fall.

When you lose your balance, resist for a long time before turning yourself toward the earth. Then jump.

You must not force yourself to stay steady. You must move forward.

You must win.

The wire trembles. The tendency is to want to calm it by force. In fact, you must move with grace and suppleness to avoid disturbing the song of the cable.

It is better to take your first steps without a balancing pole. Above all, it is natural. This cumbersome bar can help an experienced walker to make an effortless crossing, but it is utterly useless to the beginner. You should not begin to think about a balancing pole until you have mastered balancing on one foot and have been able to make a partial crossing without losing your composure.

The balancing pole is generally a wooden rod or a metal tube with a diameter that allows for easy handling; it is five to eight meters in length. Its weight varies according to the situation: the exercise balancing pole weighs twenty pounds; the balancing pole used in great crossings can be as heavy as fifty pounds. The way it is made is the wire walker's secret. Assemble your own and do not tell anyone how you did it.

So that the foot will feel the cable and not lend itself to accidental slips, buffalo-hide slippers are recommended, though in rainy weather these should be replaced by slippers with rubber soles. But any unreinforced shoes with the main sole removed, or even thick socks—several on each foot—will do the job quite well. In the same way, a twisted green branch or an old rusty pipe will be perfectly adequate for the first balancing pole.

Don't waste your time on the ground.

Work without stopping. Little by little, the wire must belong to you.

Hold the balancing pole firmly, arms spread. Never dip it. It is moved to the left, to the right, in a horizontal gesture. The body does not lean. The hips do not move. The leg is rigid without being dead. But you discover that on your own.

By the end of the day, you will have made your first crossing.

Read this!

"The equilibrist on his rope is in an unstable state of equilibrium; that is, his base of support being very narrow in the lateral sense, and his center of gravity being situated above (approximately at the level of the hollow of the

stomach), this center of gravity tends to displace itself constantly. Now, the least displacement leads to a breakdown of the force; the weight pushing vertically breaks apart into two other forces which form between them a right angle whose summit is at the center of gravity. One follows the axis of the body, the other tends to make the body pivot around the base of support; its size is equal to the angle of the body's axis. It is this force that tends to make the equilibrist fall; the talent of the equilibrist consists in never letting this force have greater power than those which he uses to destroy it."

The man who wrote these words deserves a taste of the wire!

Walking

The horseman knows the pleasure of working his horse at a slow pace. He leaves galloping to the frenzied knight.

Perfectly calm, the high-wire walker will endlessly practice "the Time of the Rope." This consists of traveling the length of his cable slowly, one step at a time. This is the first exercise with the balancing pole. It is also the most important and the most ancient. After a great number of crossings back and forth, you will know what it is to go and what it is to return. Continue to do this for a long time before attempting a real walk. For a walk on the wire must be slow and careful, like a line pulled tight by the strength of your eyes: the body straight, the foot firmly inside the wire with each step, the balancing pole motionless.

To put your whole foot on the wire all at once produces a sure though heavy kind of walking, but if you first slide your toes, then your sole, and finally your heel onto the wire, you will be able to experience the intoxicating lightness that is so magnificent at great heights. And then people will say of you: "He is strolling on his wire!" Dismount and pace off nine meters holding the balancing pole: that is the perfect walk! This test is necessary: you were beginning to feel like a high-wire walker.

Walking is the soul of the wire. There are an infinite number of styles.

There is the walk that glides, like that of a bull-fighter who slowly approaches his adversary, the presence of danger growing with each new step, his body arched outrageously, hypnotized.

There is the unbroken, continuous walk, without the least concern for balance, the pole on your shoulder, your arm swinging and your eyes turned upward, as if you were looking for your thoughts in the sky; this is the solid walk of a man of the earth returning home, a tool over his shoulder, satisfied with his day's work.

These walks happen to be mine.

Discover your own. Work on them until they are perfect.

The backward walk is not practiced.
Unless it happens to be particularly agreeable to you.

Running

Running?
Ah! Yes, running is entertaining.
It's fresh, it's tempting, it's joyous, it's distracting.
All running is joyful.
Ah! How he runs on his wire!

You are running to a certain fall.

Running will come naturally from a light and rapid
way of walking.
Let it come by itself.

When you walk, the foot follows the line of the
wire: in this way you can do extremely rapid crossings and brief runs. But to run vigorously on a cable,
you must put your feet sideways across the wire, like
a duck. To begin, run on the wire thinking only of
regularity; running will be difficult. Add speed, and
it will become impossible.

You must set your eyes so that they take in the whole length of the wire. You must feel it in space. Measure its extension. The distance is too great to hazard without courage: hold the balancing pole in front of you and take off with a sure and straight step. With the help of your open arms, clear a path for yourself, push your hips along the wire to the very end; your feet will follow, your body will get through. You want your steps to control this length of steel. Launch yourself then, and cross it with three long strides.

To understand running is to harmonize the wind of your steps with the breath of the wire—without asking questions.

Running is not the way to go quickly from one end of the wire to the other.

Running? It is the acrobat's laughter!

Running without a balancing pole is perhaps the most demanding exercise of High-Wire Art.

The quest for immobility

This is the mystery of the rope dance. The essence, the secret. Time plays no part in achieving it.

Or perhaps I should say "in approaching it."

To approach it, the high-wire walker turns himself into an alchemist. Again and again, he attempts it along the wire, but without ever entering the Domain of Immobility—where, I was told, the arms become useless, hanging alongside a body that is ten times heavier than before.

The feeling of a second of immobility—if the wire grants it to you—is an intimate happiness.

Come to the middle of the wire with the most beautiful of your walks.

Achieve a state of balance, and then wait. All by itself, the balancing pole will become horizontal, your body will settle on two fixed and solid legs.

Immobility will come promptly. Or so you would think.

You will feel yourself immobile: I'm not moving, therefore I'm immobile.

And what about your eyes that watch and wander?

I saw your eyes climbing up through the trees.

And those thoughts in your skull, stammering back and forth?

And the blood rushing through your veins? And the wind in your hair? And the bobbing wire? And all this air you eat and chew?

What a racket!

No, the tiny inhabitants of the weeds have never seen such an agitated being.

The quest for immobility is even more deceptive if you give up the balancing pole, but it is absolutely essential.

You must devote yourself to it.

Balanced on one foot, the balancing foot, slowly bring your arm and leg to rest. Hold this position. This is the first point. Then put your free leg into contact with the other, your two feet on the wire;

your arms will serve as a balancing pole, you will gradually move them less and less. This is the second point. Now you must get rid of these arms: by crossing them in front of you, by letting them hang naturally, or by putting them behind your back. All this happens in surreptitious ways. Clandestinely. This is the third point.

It is now a matter of patience. It is between the wire and you.

Approach. Feel how balance no longer exists. Be on the lookout for the moment when you will suddenly stop breathing. An otherworldly heaviness will anchor you to the cable. You will breathe along it: the air will surge from the end of the wire, work its way slowly along it, pierce the soles of your feet, climb up through your legs, inundate your body, and in the end reach your nostrils. You will exhale without any pause, and your breath will travel back along the same path: softly, from your lips, you will expel the air, and it will go down, flow around each muscle, trace the outline of your feet, and then re-enter the wire. . . .

Do not abandon your breath halfway. Pursue it

until it escapes through the end of your wire, in the same way it came.

Your breathing will become slow, distended, long like a thread.

You and the rigging will become a single body, solid as a rock.

You will feel yourself a thing of balance. You will become wire.

Once you have built this flawless balance, so fleeting and fragile, it will be as dense for you as granite.

If no thought came to disturb this miracle, it would go on and on. But man, who is astonished by everything, himself included, quickly loses hold of it.

The minute point of balance hovers above the wire, knocks against the wire walker, and navigates like a feather in the wind of his efforts.

Let this wind slacken, let it die, and the feather will soon enter the wire walker and come to rest in his center of gravity.

This is the way it happens then: first, you reach a relative calm; then, you achieve a second, finer balance; and finally, if only rarely, you attain a brief instant of absolute immobility.

For the wind of our thoughts is more violent than the wind of balance and will soon set this delicate feather fluttering again.

Barefoot

I am nostalgic for the old ropes.

You walked on them with bare feet. Not so on the cable.

How proud the tightrope walker was. On the bottom of each foot there was an astonishing tattoo, a mark made far above the crowds. It was the sign of his art and his daring, and only he knew it was there. Its hardness was proof to him that he was Emperor of the Air, and even on the ground he continued to walk on these tough, callused lines.

The foot lived well when it lived with hemp.

The steel cable has replaced the rope, and if it breathes it is only because its soul is made of hemp. And even though the foot can never merge with the metal, you must go back often to working barefoot. This is indispensable. The foot can then find its place on the cable, and the cable can find its place in the foot.

But that must be attempted delicately.

The wire penetrates between the big toe and the second toe, crosses the foot along the whole length of the sole, and escapes behind the middle of the heel. One can also make the wire enter along the bottom of the big toe; the sole is then traversed obliquely, and the cable leaves slightly to one side of the heel. If this second method is acceptable for certain walks, the first is nevertheless essential. You must be able to use the big toe and the second toe to grip the wire and hang on to it (this is the only way to avoid a slip during a Death Walk).

Remain balanced on one foot until the pain is no longer bearable, and then prolong this suffering for another minute before changing feet.

Repeat the exercise, then attempt a series of walks. Wait until the foot is perfectly placed before taking the next step.

When the positioning of each foot has become quite natural, the legs will have gained their independence, and your step will have become noble and sure.

You won't get results from a few hours of serious work. You must continue until your flesh understands it.

But I promise that when your feet slide to rest on a cable bed, you will astonish yourself with a smile of deep weariness.

Look: on your sole there is what my friend Fouad calls the Line of Laughter. It corresponds to the mark of the wire.

The high-wire walker's salute

Before entering the last phase of combat,
the bullfighter removes his *montera*
and, in a neat circling gesture, presents it to the
    crowd.
Then he throws it onto the sand.
The matador's salute is a dedication.

When the balloon is ready, the pilot orders:
    "Hands off!"
Rising above a forest of arms, he flourishes his cap
in broad figure eights and disappears.
The aeronaut's salute is a farewell.

The wire walker, after setting foot on the cable,
walks halfway across, stops, and slides down to
    one knee.
He removes one hand from his balancing pole.
The wire walker's salute is a dedication.

Of strength, of magnificence.
He thrusts his fist into the teeth of the wind,
and in the same movement his fist opens to
    receive the answer.
The wire walker reads it in his own hand, there,
    resting
on one knee, in the middle of the wire.
News of death, a promise of joy:
he lets nothing escape
of what he has learned.

Except for the Time of the Rope, the Salute is the first exercise the high-wire walker must learn.

There is the standing salute, the kneeling salute, and the sitting salute.

The first is made on one leg, balancing pole resting horizontally on the raised thigh, the arm up.
    The second is the true high-wire walker's salute. So that it will be perfect, a part of the body's weight must rest on the top of the foot where it joins the ankle, and the whole

top of the foot must be touching the cable—not just the knuckles of the foot. You often see this, and it is a disgrace.

The sitting salute is the same as the standing, except that the wire passes under the thigh and the middle of the buttocks.

You can achieve the sitting salute unexpectedly—by jumping onto the wire from the standing position. The leg muscles will absorb the vibrations of this sudden encounter with the cable.

There are numerous variations to the high-wire walker's salute.

I have discovered old engravings in which the acrobat is kneeling, but only the knee is touching the rope; the rest of the leg is in the air perpendicular to the wire.

A salute is made when you step onto the wire, but there is also the salute that concludes a performance, and as a general rule the strongest moment of any exercise can be accompanied by an appropriate salute. There is no particular salute without a balancing pole. One possibility would be to imitate those gymnasts with big mustaches who posed for the earliest cameras: standing proudly and *simply, arms crossed, head held high, feet almost at right angles, the torso inflated. I do this. I call it the Salute in the Old Style.*

But there is nothing, it seems to me, more gravely majestic than the moment when the high-wire walker, with admirable reverence, takes leave of his wire.

Exercises

Walking, running, and the salute precede a multitude of exercises; an infinite number, in fact, if one were to include all the variants. Often the balancing pole is required; sometimes special equipment must be used. One must also mention the net, the belt, and other safety systems. They guarantee the conquest of the impossible—but at the same time they cheapen the victory. A rule of thumb would be the following: anything that can be done on the ground can be done on the wire, although sometimes necessarily in a slightly different form. To draw up the complete list of exercises for rope, cable, and low wire would be as impossible as pretending to draw up a list of newly invented exercises, exercises that have not yet been done, or exercises that are unheard of, that defy execution.

Here, in any case, is a list—presented more or less in order of appearance:

The Time of the Rope. Walking.

Running.

The salute.

Dancing.

Splits.

The pretend fall.

The headstand (with or without balancing pole).

Resting on the wire, in a supine position.

The genuflection; walking while genuflecting.

Balancing on one knee.

The planche: balancing on one leg.

One-arm handstand.

The cartwheel.

Balancing, facing the audience.

High-bar exercises.

Descending an inclined cable by sliding on the stomach (a specialty of the Middle Ages); hanging from the back of the neck, or with one foot attached to a pulley.

The Death Walk (up or down an inclined cable, with or without the balancing pole).

Blindfolded: walking with the head covered, walking in a sack.

Dancing in wooden shoes.

Dancing with scythes, sickles, or daggers attached to the ankles.

Walking with feet in baskets (with wicker bottoms or fake bottoms made of cloth).

The bound walk: ankles chained together.

Jumping through a paper hoop.

Walking with a pennant, crossing with flags.

With a pitcher and glass of water: refreshments on the rope.

Walking with a candlestick or sword (the prop is balanced on the chin, the nose, or even the forehead, for the length of a balancing or, for wire walkers of great heights, for the length of a crossing with the balancing pole—without the balancing pole for slack-rope walkers).

Tricks with a Chinese umbrella or an Indian fan (often on an inclined rope).

The half-turn without the balancing pole.

The half-turn jump without the balancing pole.

The half-turn with the balancing pole (the wire walker turns; his balancing pole does not move).

Juggling (usually with balls, clubs, torches, or hoops), with or without the balancing pole. The pole can be balanced off-center on the wire with the help of the balancing foot.

Walking in a hoop. (The hoop rolls on the wire and is kept in a vertical position by the feet of the wire walker, who walks on the inside.)

Hoop around the ankles. (The hoop is kept in a horizontal position by the ankles, which means the wire walker must take broad, semicircular steps so as not to lose the hoop.)

Passing a hoop over the body and stepping out.

Walking with the balancing pole behind the back.

Walking with the balancing pole above the head, arms fully extended.

With the balancing pole on the shoulders.

Putting the balancing pole behind the back (over the shoulders or under the legs).

Walking backward.

Wearing disguises.

Imitating characters, animals.

Wearing armor.

Doing comedy routines on the wire.

Playing a musical instrument (in all positions).

Balancing on a small wooden plank (motionless, or with tiny leaps forward).

Balancing on a ladder, or on a step ladder.

Balancing on a chair, its struts or legs resting on the rope.

With a table and chair: a meal on the wire.

With a stove and kitchen equipment: cooking an
omelette on the wire.

Pistol dancing, sword dancing. Knife throwing.

Precision shooting on the wire, shooting at a moving target, shooting balloons.

On a velocipede, bicycle.

On a unicycle (regular-size, giant).

Walking on stilts.

High jumping. Hurdling a table.

Jumping rope. Double, triple, crisscross, while moving forward.

Jumping over a riding crop held in both hands,
frontward and backward.

High-wire walker's somersault (forward roll with
jump start with a balancing pole).

True somersault (feet to feet), frontward or backward (the principle exercise of low-wire artists
and ropedancers, but unthinkable for a wire
walker of great heights without protection).

The caboulot (backward roll with a balancing pole).
Crossing the wire with caboulots.

The reverse (a caboulot without the balancing pole
in which the acrobat takes hold of the cable behind him from a lying position and pulls, which

rolls him over backward and puts him in a sitting
position).

The human load (carrying someone on your back);
the "baptism of wire" (taking someone from the
audience and putting him on the wire for the first
time); pushing a wheelbarrow with someone in
it.

Falling astride the wire (usually to initiate a series
of caboulots).

Spinning around the wire, starting from a strad-
dling position.

Balancing a perch on the forehead, with crossing.

Hanging: from the knees, ankles, or toes.

Tightrope acts on a slack wire attached below the
main cable.

The high-bar catch-and-swing. (After a real or
feigned slip, the wire walker, hanging by his
hands, gets back onto the wire by flaring out his
legs over it; as soon as his feet catch hold of the
wire, he turns around it, before springing to a
standing position.)

Fireworks shot off on the wire (knapsack filled with
sand in which fuses have been planted; helmet
with a pinwheel; balancing pole adorned with
flares and catherine wheels—lighted with a ciga-

rette at the middle of the wire). This exercise is often fatal.

Jumping on one foot, with crossing.

Crossing a burning wire (with boots and asbestos clothes).

"True" crossing on a motorcycle (holding the balancing pole, with no counterweight under the machine).

"False" crossing on a motorcycle (with a trapeze that works as a counterweight and holds the machine on the cable).

Exercises with a partner, group exercises:

The human column, either stationary or advancing along the wire (two, three, or four people on the shoulders of the under-stander).

The human column on a unicycle, on a bicycle (with two or three people).

The bicycle with trapeze hanging below the wheels (one or two trapezes).

The human pyramid (metal bars—"forks"—create a scaffolding for three, four, five, six, seven, eight, or nine people).

A pyramid of three bicycles, with crossing.

Two people passing each other from opposite directions, without a balancing pole, by "ducking" (without touching), by "embracing" (grabbing the partners' hands and turning while leaning outward).

Passing the sleeper. (You cross your partner, who is lying down on the cable, by placing your foot on his stomach.)

Passing the sleeper by jumping over him.

Jumping over the seated partner.

Passing with a balancing pole (with the partner seated, or lying down).

Climbing on the partner's back, then shoulders, and leaping forward, to land feet first on the wire.

Backward somersault *(salto mortale)* from the shoulders of an under-stander to the shoulders of another (never done without a safety belt).

Jumping from a springboard or teeterboard attached to the cable and landing on the under-stander's shoulders.

The Ladder of Death. (In the beginning, a simple ladder was placed flat across the wire, with one acrobat at each end. Today, the ladder is solidly attached to the cable and can freely pivot around it.)

The human belt. (The body of the rider is wrapped around the waist of the under-stander.)

The human wheelbarrow. (The rider has his legs attached to the waist of the carrier and holds a wheel in his hands that he guides along the wire.)

Head to head.

Head to foot. (The top mounter stands on the under-stander's head.)

The wire walker's somersault (forward caboulot) over one, two, three, or four people.

Working with several wires at different heights and angles.

Working with a wire that changes heights and angles during the act.

Working with animals as partners (bears, monkeys, birds).

It is also important to mention the roles of the various kinds of wires:

There are exercises for low-wire artists and ropedancers that cannot be done on a high-wire walker's cable; others can be done on any kind of wire. It is obvious that an acrobat on a slack rope one and a half meters from the ground can raise his eyes for a long time to keep an object balanced on his forehead or to juggle; the high-wire walker, on a cable without elasticity or movement, can do no more than attempt the same exercise without a balancing pole. He will never succeed, however, unless he has immense talent.

The high-wire walker must be an inventor.

Jean-François Gravelet, a.k.a. Charles Blondin, prepared an omelette on the wire; he also opened a bottle of champagne and toasted the crowd. He even managed to take photographs—from the middle of the wire—of the crowd that was watching him cross the rapids at Niagara Falls.

Madame Saqui created historical frescoes to the glory of Emperor Napoleon, all by herself on the tightrope.

Rudy Omankowsky, Jr., set off numerous fireworks from his cable. He specialized in somersaulting from a bicycle over four people (the bike would fall into the net at the moment of takeoff). His father, "Papa Rudy" Omankowsky, taught him the extraordinary dismount from the giant unicycle: jumping forward onto the cable. He himself was the master of a series of caboulots—his legs now shooting out to the right, now to the left, now on either side of the wire—and performed a dramatic crossing in a sack that ended with straddle falls and a series of rolls.

The ventriloquist Señor Wences has told me that on the tightrope, "facing the audience," Miguel Robledillo imitated a staggering drunk.

Francis Brunn, the legendary juggler, remembers admiringly how Alzana would jump rope on wet cables and continue to jump even after he had lost balance and was being carried away from the axis of the wire.

I myself have witnessed the delicate crossings of Sharif Magomiedoff several times: he places the tip of his wife's foot on his forehead and walks along the wire while keeping her balanced—she herself is protected from falling by a safety belt. My friend Pedro Carillo goes down the steepest walk by jumping without a balancing pole and, almost in total darkness, slides down—sometimes backward—to reach the ground.

As for myself, I am endlessly hunting for new exercises—like throwing away the balancing pole; the half-turn with balancing pole sweeping through space; walking on tiptoe so as not to wake up the sleeping circus; bouncing a ball on my forehead; and other juggling acts directly inspired by Francis Brunn.

And, lest I forget the masters of us all: the high-wire animals. Artists have painted them with great enthusiasm, and photographs have allowed us to know the truth that lurks behind the legends.

Walking in wicker baskets is an old and very pleasant exercise. A great family of wire walkers robbed a cigarette manufacturer in this way.

It all happened long ago, so perhaps the story can now be told.

Once, while performing outdoors, they attached one end of their rope to the window of a cigarette warehouse. Having come to the basket exercise in their performance, the wire walkers repeated it so many times that the audience, which did not share this excessive passion for baskets, began to hoot with impatience.

The baskets were being systematically loaded at one end of the wire and then carefully emptied at the other. In this way, the family managed to steal enough cigarettes to fill a hay cart.

Without a balancing pole

This is the foundation of the art of high-wire walking.

For safety reasons, however, the high-wire walker has forgotten it.

It is rare to see a high-wire walker at great heights without a balancing pole.

It is, however, the purest image of a man on a line.

In a crossing without balancing pole, we see the qualities of an acrobat; in a true performance without balancing pole, we salute the blood of the high-wire walker.

The succession of balancings—first on one foot and then on the other—that allowed you to move along the wire with skill must now be developed into a controlled walk. The crossing must be made at an even speed, without the slightest loss of equilibrium.

If before you had to fix your eyes on the cable several yards in front of you, now you must look all the way to the end. This connection with the "target" is obligatory, and more than once it has saved a life.

Running without a balancing pole can be attempted only after your walk has become infallible. You can master it with constant and devoted work over a number of years. Like a juggler, you must practice fiercely and without distraction. Otherwise, your attempts on the wire will remain attempts, and you will always lose.

For example, consider the half-turn:

You can have an exact idea of it without ever being able to do it successfully.

Create a vertical motion in the wire; the moment to attempt the half-turn is when the wave is at its maximum height; the body will be lighter, the feet will turn more easily. This wave is imperceptible. Press down harder with the back foot; it will serve as a pivot. Remember that the feet never completely leave the wire during a half-turn.

To turn around on both legs at once, you must raise yourself slightly on the balls of your feet; the heels swivel one hundred and eighty degrees to meet up with the wire again at the same time as the front part of your feet. The half-turn can be done to the right or the left, after coming to a full stop or in the middle of a walk. This last will come as a surprise—like a sleepwalker suddenly changing direction.

If I had to present myself in the Paradise of Rope Dancers by doing one walk, and one walk only, I would make my entrance without a balancing pole. I would walk as naturally as possible, my arms at my sides, letting them sway slightly to the rhythm of my step. I would walk straight ahead without thinking for a single moment that I was on a wire: like some passerby receding into the distance.

And my salute would be a one-knee balancing without pole—which I believe is something no one has ever done before.

The king poles

The high-wire walker no longer lives among the low branches of the trees. A new wire is waiting for him.

A solid gray wire, perhaps fifteen meters long, stretched out six or eight meters above the ground between two poles painted in the performer's favorite color. On these poles the wire walker can rest, place his different balancing poles, store his chair or his bicycle, as well as his juggling clubs and unicycle. The platform floor should be a square of wood strong enough to support all the equipment and the aerialist himself. It is positioned below the cable. The platforms of low-wire artists and ropedancers are positioned above the cable. They step down onto their cable. The high-wire walker, however, steps up onto his. Along the vertical axis of the walk cable, and on each side, an ungreased cable is stretched down to the ground.

One of these inclined cables is drawn out to maximum length for the Death Walk. It is along this path that you will climb up to the installation, unless you have the patience to build a hemp-rope ladder with oak rungs.

Each pole is held vertically by the "obseclungs"—two thin cables attached to the top of the pole that come down perpendicular to the walk line and form a forty-five-degree angle with the ground. These guy wires are pulled into place by pulleys attached with "beckets" to "stakes." The whole installation is thus anchored by the stakes, thick steel bars—formerly wooden bars—that are driven into the ground with sledgehammers. These in turn have a sling of steel or hemp attached to them. This is called the becket.

Putting up the king poles will be your first great joy as a high-wire walker.

You measure the terrain. In the designated spots you lay out the pole sections that you will later fit together; these are hollow tubes or trussed pylons. Then you proceed to the "dressing": one by one jibing the platforms and poles with all their cables, in an order so complicated that the neophyte will have to go through it several times before he can assume sole responsibility for it. It goes without saying that you must have won the friendship of an old high-wire walker who will share his rigging secrets with you, and that he is with you now. If not, you will have to go about it according to your own ideas, and sooner or later you will pay for it with your life.

When the equipment is ready, you drive in the stakes. If five men produce a series of strokes in rapid succession—"a flying five"—watch out for the pieces of steel that whistle down, to land in a tree trunk twenty feet away, or in the flesh of a man who was not paying attention.

You raise up the king poles. One after the other. With the aid of a six-sheave block and tackle. Then you attach the tightening device: a heavy chain hoist or a giant turnbuckle. This latter should not be used for a big installation if the longitudinal section of the screw forms a series of triangles, for it wears out and gives way. The screw should have a square shape so that it will never loosen. This is the kind of turnbuckle used for coupling railroad cars.

The curvature of the wire changes according to the height. Soon it will trace a straight line that seems rigorous; you then attach the cavalletti to the blocks and give a final turn to the tightening device—the "pull to death"—just before beginning your work.

To give your routines on the wire an aspect of perfection and to execute highly delicate balancings, the cable must not buckle or sway between the two poles. To avoid this, you attach a thin plate of light metal over the walk cable at appropriate intervals. These plates will fit snugly over the wire. To each flap you attach a length of hemp, the same thickness as the walk cable, that will be drawn down to the ground from various points on the wire at the same angle as the obseclungs. These are the cavallettis. The shape of the plates allows a bicycle rim to pass over them without jumping off track; because of the thickness of the ropes that secure them, you will not find yourself on the ground looking at your own severed arm after an accidental slip—which happened to an artist who had chosen to use a thin steel wire.

At times the cavallettis require these plates; at other times they do not. The cavallettis are necessary for great crossings and preferable for "high work" between the poles; in the open air, they are generally spaced fifteen meters apart. But Blondin, who worked on rope, placed them at every two meters for difficult crossings.

For a fifteen-meter wire between two poles, two cavallettis will be acceptable. Obviously, when there are too many cavallettis or when they are too close to one another, we sense the amateurism and cowardice of the performer. If you want to avoid the slightest jolt on the cable, if you want to be certain that it will not vibrate as you go over the cavallettis, at the end of each rope you must use a pulley and attach a counterweight—a bag of sand or a bucket of water. The rope crosses through the pulley, which is attached two meters from the ground by a brace anchored to a chain that in turn is tied to a stake. The wire will then breathe with each of your steps without giving way or turning.

All this must be learned. You cannot make it up.

There are some high-wire walkers who would rather die with their knowledge than let newcomers learn it. Besides, circus people distrust anyone who does not "live on the road," and how could it be otherwise?

The length of the walk cable should always exceed ten meters; the length works as a function of the height of the poles. For six-meter poles, a good length is twelve meters. A number of aerialists would say fifteen meters; this makes the installation easier, since the circus ring measures thirteen and a half meters in diameter and the poles are always placed just outside the ring. The more one stretches the line without raising the height, the lower the installation will seem. And vice versa.

The high-wire walker eagerly carries his balancing pole to the foot of the king poles. With a smile he abandons the "little wire" of his first crossings. From now on, he will return to it only to learn new exercises or to throw himself into some whirling caper he hopes to invent. He puts his foot on the inclined cable and scales the sky, where the motionless birds are waiting to meet him.

Alone on his wire

Up above, about to begin a long acquaintance with his new territory, the high-wire walker feels himself alone. His body will remain motionless for a long time. Grasping the platform with both hands behind him, he stands before the cable, as if he did not dare set foot on it.

It looks as though he is idly basking in the setting sun.

Not at all. He is buying time.

He measures space, feels out the void, weighs distances, watches over the state of things, takes in the position of each object around him. Trembling, he savors his solitude. He knows that if he makes it across, he will be a high-wire walker.

He wants to line up his doubts and fears with his thoughts—in order to hoist up the courage he has left.

But that takes too much time.

The cable grows longer, the sky becomes dark, the other platform is now a hundred meters away. The ground is no longer in the same place; it has moved even lower. Cries come from the woods. The end of the day is near.

At the deepest moment of his despair, feeling he must now give up, the high-wire walker grabs his balancing pole and moves forward. Step by step, he crosses over.

This is his first accomplishment.

He stands there trying to absorb it, his eyes blankly staring at this new platform, while darkness skims over the ground.

With the tops of the trees he shares the day's last light, a light softer than air.

Alone on his wire, he wraps himself more deeply in a wild and scathing happiness, crossing helter-skelter into the dampness of the evening. He attaches his balancing pole to the platform before settling down at the top of the mast. There, in a corner of dark and chilly space, he waits calmly for the night to come.

Practice

The shock of it lasted several days.

Every morning he ran to his wire, leaping over the grass so the dew would not weigh him down. Distracted by so much happiness, he would let himself simply walk back and forth, again and again. There are those who think this coming and going will turn them into high-wire walkers. The true man of the wire, however, cannot accept this horizontal monotony for very long: he knows that the path he is about to take has no limit. In remembrance of his recent birth, he stops short and sets to work. Silent and alone, he brings to the high cable everything he has learned down below. He discards the movements space will not support and gathers up the others into a group that he will polish, refine, lighten, and bring closer and closer to himself.

Each day he adds another mastered element.

Soon he goes out on his wire with only one goal:

to discover new ideas, to invent a combination of unexpected gestures. He goes out hunting. And what he catches he hangs on his wire. Then he distracts himself with inconsequential walks, whimsical postures, exercises with no future, like a bear wallowing in his pool at the zoo. And if he loses his taste for movement to such an extent that he loses control, better that he should rest on the wire than stop and climb down. For you must reach some apex before stepping to the ground, no matter how small it is: your existence as a high-wire walker is at stake. You must leave the wire in triumph, not out of weariness.

Now that he knows how to go about practicing, each session will be longer, more fruitful, and the day will be meaningless unless it bears the shape of the wire.

Then the music starts!

For stimulation, he turns on the brassiest Circassian marches; he draws courage from Spanish bullfighting music; and, with exquisite ardor, he surrounds himself with the sound of a full orchestra.

The wire walker at rest

At the time when wire walkers stretched their ropes between two X's of wood, one of the X's was always reserved for resting.

There was a simple hemp line stretched between the tops of the two beams, high enough for the dancer to lean the small of his back against it. It was covered by a large cloth decorated in the artist's colors and embroidered with fine gold threads. Leaning against it in this way, the acrobat could indifferently let his eyes wander down to settle on the rope.

As his name indicates, the wire walker of great heights is a dreamer: he has another way of resting. He stretches out on his cable and contemplates the sky. There he gathers his strength, recovers the serenity he may have lost, regains his courage and his faith. But weariness is necessary: you must not treat resting as an exercise.

Sit down. Fold one leg on the cable and then lean backward until your head touches it. A moment later the foot will begin to slide, and the leg will stretch out completely; the other leg will hang down and sway. Sometimes one hand lets go of the pole; sometimes it retrieves it. You want to feel the line of the wire. It will become your spinal column. Each passing second shrieks like a grindstone. An endless pain takes hold of your body and breaks it down muscle by muscle. If you resist and cross the threshold of what is bearable, the torture will extend into your bones and break them one by one across the wire. You will be a skeleton balanced on a razor blade. Beyond this limit, millions of terrifying enchantments await you. Beyond this limit, breath and confidence go together. And still further beyond, a patience without desire will give each of your thoughts its real density.

Then be lazy—to the point of delirium!

With your back on the wire, you feel the vastness of the sky. To be a wire walker in its profoundest sense means to leave the wire behind you, to discover the cables that have been strung even higher and, step by step, to reach the Magic Wire of Immobility, the

Wire that belongs to the Masters of the World. The earth itself rests on it. It is the Wire that links the finite to the infinite: the straightest, shortest path between one star and the next.

Now close your eyes.

The cable is limpid. Your body is silent. Together, they are motionless. Only your leg quivers. You would like to cut it off, to turn your body into a single human wire. But already it no longer belongs to you, is no longer a part of you. Like the chess player who closes his eyes and sees a whole plain of black and white squares passing under his feet, you close your eyes and see only a magnificent gray wire.

The silent wind of your eyes inhabits it.

A silence invaded by light.

Penetrate this luminosity by seeking out its source. Plunge down to find the place where nothing breathes, into the blackness that is hidden inside it. Keep going until you reach the other side of the light. It is a dazzling clarity, a clamorous splendor: wet, whirling, often colorless. As if through a black mirror, you will see a gleaming, untouched wire. That is the image you are looking for. It will quickly be jumbled together with the fireworks of new impressions. Once this image has come, however, the high-wire walker can live in space. For whole hours, for portions of entire days, as if time had come to a halt. No one else will ever notice.

You must throw yourself into this meaningless search for rest—without hoping for a result.

Here is the wire walker stretched out on his gigantic antenna, listening to the world. He can feel the noise of the city rise up to him; he can distinguish among the thousand sounds that fill the silence of the countryside. He starts at the whistling of shooting stars.

And all that puts him to sleep.

A deep breathing invades him.

Each time he draws in his breath, he hears noises; each time he exhales, he hears nothing. Then, during the space of several heartbeats, he forgets everything. He begins to snore. But between his sighs, what silence!

Below him, nothing. Neither dogs nor people. Nature has gone to sleep as well, so that the wire walker, balanced on his huge tuning fork, can at last begin to dream.

The blindfolded Death Walk

You have no idea what's in store for you.

A cable inclined at a thirty-degree angle. From the ground to the top of the pole or the church bell tower. Three hundred meters. Guy-lined at intervals by a few lengths of hemp. Swaying in the face of a drowsing sun.

Despite all the care that has been given to its installation, the wire will never demark an evenly ascending line. It will dip into space, become horizontal at low altitudes, gently raise its head, lift up its nose, and with growing malice mime a venomous verticality in its last section.

When a blindfolded Death Walk takes place, it is always announced as an "attempt."

Step by step you will climb up, your eyes pressed against the black cloth, your face buried in the suffocating sack. Blind, deaf, and dumb, you will doubt you can reach the end of the wire.

The sun, which has been beating down since dawn, has drawn out the grease hidden in the soul of the cable. With your first steps, the whole installation will begin to move. Each cavalletti will pull on its area—which will amplify the wire's oscillation, as if it were now trying to throw you off. Without ever knowing where they are, your feet will unexpectedly touch an oily spot—and you will advance by millimeters, your hands clutching the balancing pole. The one you have chosen is long and heavy, and with each step forward it will grow even heavier. You will be at the end of your strength when the abrupt angle of the last steps begins, and the wind will be waiting in ambush for you there. You will think you are in the middle of the wire, so you will kneel down for an impeccable aerialist's salute, which will be ridiculous, for in fact you will be only ten meters from your starting point. You will lengthen your strides with the thought that you are half finished with the crossing, and you will bang your body into the pole or a stone of the building, for the walk is over. Then, with a superb gesture, you will tear off the blindfold and the hood, almost falling with the last step, for your vertigo will be total as you stand in the sudden dazzling light of the sun.

The first ascent will remain the most vivid sensation in your life as a high-wire walker. You will think: My shadow was faithful, it has led me this far, and if by chance courage fails me, I will throw the corpse of my memories helter-skelter on the wire, and in this way reach the heart of a storm that will allow me to scale these ferocious heights.

Fakes

I know a man who sells himself body and soul to the highest bidder.

He uses a blindfold with holes in it, an immense balancing pole that hangs over both sides of his overly guy-lined wire, and presents his exercises above a net. He has learned how to walk on the cable with an "extension cord"—a second wire that runs parallel to the one he walks on. It is just above his head, and he can grab onto it whenever he wants.

Over the circus rings where he works as a so-called high-wire walker, he uses a "mechanic." This is an almost invisible cable attached to a safety belt that has been sewn into his costume. His assistant, who stays on the ground during his performance, manipulates the string with tiny, discrete movements, as though he were controlling a puppet. As a result, this equilibrist is able to do stunts that no wire walker could ever attempt, much less accomplish. Three times I saw him do a backward somersault on an inclined wire: this is impossible. Three times I saw him fail to gain his footing. Three times I saw his body fall to one side of the wire—although this was imperceptible to the crowd—and three times I saw his balance righted by the safety line. The rest of his performance was punctuated by cries, feigned slips, and pretend falls. From the simplest, most limpid exercises he knew how to extract interminable difficulties, which he mimed in the most grotesque fashion. Before he stepped onto the wire, he would take great care to rub the soles of his shoes with resin powder. Thus, his feet were not placed on the wire, they were glued to it. When I had the chance to walk on his wire, I could not take a step: my feet got stuck. I am used to wearing old and extremely smooth slippers so my walks will be as lithe and graceful as possible.

The terrain of the high-wire walker is bounded by death, not by props. And when a wire walker inspires pity, he deserves death ten times over.

Anyone can use a net, an extension cord, a blindfold with holes in it, a trick balancing pole, resin, cavallettis that touch each other, and a mechanic.

To make life even sweeter for these people, I would advise them to practice falling as well. In the realm of the Absurd, they would become the masters of every artifice.

True high-wire walkers do not do such things.

But I know another aerialist.

He often appears on the wire of my dreams.

He is immense in his red-and-black cape—which he throws down to the crowd with a giant's laughter following his first crossing. At times he is majestic. He does the simplest exercises, even the ones that other artists disdain. But he performs them with such finesse, such cunning and ease, that everything about them seems difficult. At other times, he acts like a clown, makes false steps, tangles his feet, and stops in the middle of a move to strike a comic, ridiculous pose. At still other times, he is wild, throwing himself into mad stunts without even trying to succeed. He attacks the wire, slips, catches himself, bangs his head and howls, foams, springs back.

He is alone, like a flame, and the music of his blood silences all our cheers.

But he can hear what the people in the first row are whispering:

"Isn't he charming?"

"Do you think he's going to fly?"

Murderers!

At that point, he wipes off his sweat with the back of his arm and spits into the arena.

The customer is always right!

With dash and daring he responds disdainfully by pretending to slip with each step, stunning the many spectators who have no idea what he is doing. Then he reaches his platform with classic grace, the perfection he can achieve whenever he wants to.

Laughing, I stand up to applaud him.

I allow him everything. Whatever he does I will accept.

And if he would like to start working with a net, well, maybe I wouldn't disapprove.

Then there was the inventor who came up with a counterweight for high-wire walkers.

It was nothing more than the stabilizer-trapeze of the wire walker's motorcycle, designed for a human being.

A few little wheels placed on the cable held a bundle of bricks that extended below the walker, which allowed him to rest his balancing pole discreetly on the T bar that moved before him. The apparatus was connected to the other side by a thin steel cable pulled by a winch operated carefully by an assistant. No cavallettis! The installation was therefore several tons lighter than usual. As a result, the wire could be thin, which cut the setup time and the difficulties of installation in half. The wind became less of a threat, the wire did not sway, and, above all, distance did not count. Our hero could thus fill many fine pages in the record books. Those records are make-believe. But believe them if you wish.

And then, I would be failing in my job if I did not give brief mention to the name-stealers.

After my crossing between the towers of the World Trade Center in New York, a young wire walker started performing under my name: Philippe Petit. I learned of this after he had been hired to do his act under the roof of a large department store in Paris.

My impulse to murder him has been transformed by time into a smile of pity.

But what would have been the reaction of the Great Blondin, Hero of Niagara, if he had met any of the usurpers of his name: Arsène Blondin, Hero of the Seine; Little Blondin; the Female Blondin; the Australian Blondin; and the countless Blondinis?

Wisdom says he would have been honored.

The performance

As the days went on, I found that I could repeat the same steps, the same movements.

My work was becoming serious.

I would begin with several crossings "to build confidence." But I was eager to get to what I love to do best: the slowest walks; the simplest, most delicate routines.

It was in a meadow at the end of a day of hard training that I found my first spectator, who had no doubt been attracted by my silence.

Before leaving the wire, I had allowed myself to do a crossing with one foot dragging behind me, thinking of all the things that foot might be able to do.

Suddenly, the tall hedge behind me opened.

A huge cow's head had just placed itself noiselessly on a row of brambles, its muzzle calm, its eye friendly.

Bashful at being surprised during my exercises, I withdrew very softly to the platform and then set out straight and erect to the middle of the cable, where I performed a mathematically exact half-turn and kneeled to my visitor in the most perfect fashion.

I continued to do the best and most beautiful things I knew. I did the exercises in the order I had prepared them during my practice sessions; I added what a man of the wire thinks he possesses: the expansiveness of movement, the steadiness of eye, the feeling of victory, the humor of gestures. I climbed down from the wire, covered with sweat, unable to remember having once taken a breath, while the enormous animal turned around, chewing slowly, and went back to her pasture.

Since then, I have added much to this improvised group of exercises, and I have eliminated much. With great effort, I have tried to get rid of everything superfluous. With great regret, I have kept only one salute for every ten I have practiced. I have dressed myself in white. I have had multicolored music played that was originally composed for old circuses; I have invited concert pianists to perform. My act lasts twelve minutes, even though my head is filled with centuries of wire walking.

But when I present myself on the ground and grab hold of the rope ladder or cross a public square to begin a Death Walk without a balancing pole, when I see all the equipment on the ground ready to serve me, when I see the orchestra conductor waiting for my signal, I already feel myself to be a wire walker. From that point on, it is a piece of my life that I give or abandon—it depends. The only things I ever remember are walking on the ground, taking hold of the balancing pole for the first crossing, the moment of doubt, and the final salute. I prefer the ground to be flat, uniform, uncluttered, and clean; and I make sure that the spectators have been moved out of the way.

The rest does not belong to me.

It lives in the thousands of hands that will applaud. When I hear the sound of those hands, I am the only one who knows that in the middle of my

performance, when I lie down without my balancing pole, my chest in a sky of spotlights, or my heart
open to the wind in an outdoor theater, I am next to
the gates of Paradise.

Rehearsal

Stop your normal practicing.

Keep doing walks until your leg breathes and your foot becomes a part of the wire.

Break down each element of your performance in any order you choose and examine it harshly. If the quality is good, repeat it simply as many times as necessary: you must imprint an irreproachable movement on the cable.

Make even the slightest gesture important; do not dawdle over something that seems right. Forget no part of the act.

You are now ready to rehearse.

Go down and rest. Change your costume. Prepare the music. Decide whether you want a few people to watch. Then, as if someone has just announced your entrance, walk toward the wire quickly and with a sure step.

Give your performance.

Go down, and that's it.

Do not do one more thing after that; do not amuse yourself.

Rehearse your act every day, at the end of each practice session.

And go home looking at the ground, thinking of nothing, nothing at all.

Struggle on the wire

You must throw yourself onto the wire.

Robledillo became one of the great rope dancers at the end of a whip. His father attached little bells to the wire and would come running whenever it became silent.

The glory of suffering does not interest me.

Besides, I don't believe in anything. Uselessness is the only thing I like.

Limits, traps, impossibilities are indispensable to me. Every day I go out to look for them. I believe the whip is necessary only when it is held by the student, not the teacher.

When you train, you should be outside, on a rough coast, all alone.

To learn what you must, it is important to have been treacherously overturned by the ocean's salty air. To have climbed back up to the wire with a wild leap. To have frozen yourself with rage, to have been hell-bent on keeping your balance in the claws of the wind.

You must have weathered long hours of rain and storm, have cried out with joy after each flash of lightning, have cried cries that could push back the thunder.

You must struggle against the elements to learn that staying on a wire is nothing. What counts is this: to stay straight and stubborn in your madness. Only then will you defeat the secrets of the wire. It is the most precious strength of the high-wire walker.

I have kicked off snow with every step as I walked along a frozen cable.

In other seasons, I have run barefoot over a cable burning with sunlight. I have worked without cavallettis on a big cable. I have continued walking on a cable that was progressively loosening with each step. I have tried to cross a completely loose wire, forcing myself to abandon my great assurance. I have even asked people to shake the installation with ropes, to strike the wire with long bars. . . . With complete horror and shame I have fought not to find myself hanging by one hand from the wire with the balancing pole in the other.

I have put on wooden shoes, boots, unmatched pairs of shoes. I have held my balancing pole at my side like a suitcase; I have weighted it down, lightened it, cut it in half, used it with its point off-center in order to walk leaning to one side. I have waited for darkness, so my balance would be disturbed. I have tried Death Walks that were too steep, I have groped along a greasy cable, I have played with telephone wires and railway cables. I have forced myself to rehearse with music that disgusts me. In secret, I have practiced naked to learn how the muscles work and to feel my own ridiculousness.

And, drunk with alcohol, I have proved that a body that knows what it is doing does not need a mind to lead it. . . . I have picked myself up from each of my experiments even more savagely determined. And if I fell, it was in silence. I did not wait for my shoulder wound to heal to go on with my backward somersaults—again and again and again.

I was not possessed. I was busy winning.

You do not do a true *salto* on a very high cable. You do not wear a blindfold or raise your eyes to the sky without using a balancing pole. You do not do a headstand on a great cable without a balancing pole.

Impossible?

Who is smart enough to prove it?

I tell everyone that I will attempt a crossing from the American to the Canadian side of Niagara Falls—where the water actually falls—and not over the rapids, where all previous crossings have been made. But once on that mile of unknown cable, shaken by the wind that does not stop, wrapped in a cloud of vapor that must be pierced little by little, over the whirlpools of the cataract, listening to all that infernal noise, will I dare? Will I dare to be harder than the sun, more glacial than the snow? Will I dare to enter these pages on high-wire walking without knowing the way out? It is one thing to talk about my controlled experiments. But this?

Man of the Air, illuminate with your blood the Very Rich Hours of your passage among us. Limits exist only in the souls of those who do not dream.

The wind

If this man standing at the edge of the seawall has not moved for such a long time, it is because he is looking out at the raging sea and watching the birds attempt to fly over the narrow passage—for no other reason than to intoxicate themselves with pleasure.

The harbor is deserted. The hurricane is approaching.

A mass of liquid wind, engulfed between the two towers, carries everything along with it.

The birds that cross from one wall to the next are sometimes assaulted by gusts that shut their wings with a sudden dry noise, hurling them and crushing them against a rock, where they remain until a higher and blacker wave comes to peel them off and wash them away.

The terns, the gulls—excellent sailors with voices so powerful they can hear each other through storms—have taken refuge high up in the green sky and remain silent.

Why do some of them dive down and pierce the smoking sea water that has now risen up in furious columns?

Why do they clamor and brush against the havoc of wind, dust, and foam—which they know is deadly?

Who urges this cruel-eyed animal to test himself against the storm?

One of them has almost managed to get through the forbidden passage on his back; the torrent pursues him and brings him down with a volley of hail.

Only one has made it. The gale has stripped off a few of his feathers, but he rejoins his companions, and they will make him their leader, crying out his victory until nightfall.

But he, the wire walker of the waves, knows that he was granted a miracle, and he remembers that moment with fear, for tomorrow he will be the one they discover stretched out on the seawall.

His dust feeds the wind that little by little wipes him away. Nothing is stronger than the wind. No one is stronger than the wind.

Not even the courageous bird.

The wind can make crossings on a bicycle or a unicycle extremely perilous. You must therefore use your biggest balancing pole.

As for working without a balancing pole in high winds: it is a descent into hell.

Falls

A fall from the wire, an accident up above, a failed exercise, a false step—all this comes from a lack of concentration, a badly placed foot, an exuberant overconfidence.

You must never forgive yourself.

The high-wire walker becomes the spectator of his own fall. With wide-open eyes he whirls around the wire—until he is caught by an arm or finds himself hanging by a knee. Without letting go of the balancing pole, he must take advantage of this motion to stand up again and continue the interrupted movement with rejuvenated energy.

More often than not, there will be applause. No one will understand what has happened.

The mistake is to leave without hope, without pride, to throw yourself into a routine you know will fail.

Every thought on the wire leads to a fall.

Accidents caused by equipment must not happen.

Many wire walkers have died in this way. It is stupid. But sometimes the wire slips away from you, because you have put yourself outside the law, outside the law of balance. At such moments, your survival depends on the strength of your instinct.

There are those who allow themselves to be carried away without a struggle. Let them fall!

Others continue to flail their arms and legs above the wire, to beg their eyes not to lose sight of their target. With an avid hand they latch onto the cable at the last instant. Have you ever made a leap of faith toward a distant rope, grabbed hold of a cavalletti in midair?

I waited for my first slip in public. It fortified me, it flooded me with a joyous pride, in the same way a solid clap on the shoulder encourages more than it hurts.

The second slip made me think; I found myself below the wire after completing a movement I had mastered long ago.

The third incident was terrifying: I almost fell.

Nevertheless, in my dreams I pursue legendary aerial escapes that will finally do me justice. I, who have everything to lose. For when a man begins to tremble for his life, he begins to lose it.

I demand to be allowed to end my life on the wire. I have the patience of those who have fallen once, and whenever someone tells me of a high-wire walker who fell to the ground and was crushed, I answer:

"He got what he deserved."

For that is clearly the fate and the glory of the aerial acrobat.

Great crossings

For two weeks, the high-wire walker has been camping at the top of the mountain.

It is decided. Today he will determine the anchor points.

Eagles wheel around in the lukewarm air of the gorge. They can see this little character on the peak, pointing to a spot on the facing mountain.

An enormous roll of cable is on its way. The special convoy has reached the first steep curves. It will arrive tomorrow. A thousand meters of degreased, twenty-five-millimeter wire: discovered by miracle. It is the most beautiful thing I have ever touched. It weighs three tons. I am happy.

On one side I will encircle an outcrop of rock that stands as solid as a mill.

On the other side there is no protruberance. I will have to dig a hole and then pour a broad and deep column of concrete, around which the wire will be coiled and then fastened for safety to three large trees lined up behind it.

The reel has been solidly rooted to the ground.

A team of twenty men hauls up the wire, chanting as they pull. The cable advances a few inches each minute.

It snakes along the side of the mountain. It clears the road and passes over the telegraph lines. It must be taken across the lake by high-wire methods, for no motorboat would be strong enough to pull it from one shore to the other. If the cable touches bottom, you can forget about your crossing, since it will wedge in among the rocks and catch hold of the weeds so diligently that even the most powerful machines or the most expert divers will never be able to dislodge it. It is cruel for a high wire to drown. Eventually, it will be dragged down through the forest, where each tree is an obstacle; then it will climb, foot by foot, minute after minute, toward its anchor point. At last, everything is ready.

The cable is fastened on each peak. That takes a day. It runs along the valley floor, imprinting its weight on dead leaves, drawing an almost invisible boundary. This becomes alarming at the edges of the lake. You see the black serpent dive into the water and find it hard to imagine that it will emerge on the other side, coming up into the grass and continuing on its way, marking this corner of earth with the disagreeable stamp of its metal skin. Like an immense trap, waiting to snap.

You begin to pull, aided by the largest hoist in the world—or several strategically placed pulleys—and you see a long gray line lift itself from the ground and rise up, swaying. The wire suddenly stops. A small branch somewhere is blocking it.

When you have moved the branch aside with your hand, the cable will jerk up violently another five yards. Everything will go well until the next incident. If you must go through a pine forest, you can expect an additional ten days of installation work. You will have to bend back every branch of every tree the wire gets tangled in.

Finally, the cable is over the valley. It rises up in stages. You must load the motorcycle-trapeze with two thousand pounds of cavallettis and put them astride the cable one by one, while the wire sways back and forth over a radius of ten meters.

"Tighten it to death," your ears open to every sound. Then collect your thoughts.

On the day of the crossing, you will assign each volunteer his rope—which he will have to hold and pull on with all his strength when you are above him, and which he cannot release until you have come to the next cavalletti.

Even so, the cable will move so much that you will see undulations up ahead of you in the distance. You will have to wait for each one of them to come to you before going on with your walk: feet planted, on the alert.

The sun will draw the grease out of the cable.

The wind will pick up the moment you begin.

You will have forgotten to bring socks for the end of the walk, and so you will have to go barefoot, trying to complete the crossing by grasping the wire between your first two toes at every step.

But you will not be aware of anything that is happening. You will be completely engrossed in your crossing.

Only a man who is a high-wire walker to his very bones would dare to do this.

Once on your way, you are becoming the Man of the Wire, the Magician of High Altitudes: the length of your path will be sacred to you.

When you are above the lake, do not look at the

surface of the water, for the movement of the waves will make you lose your balance.

If you manage to succeed, don't boast of it. What you have done is enough in itself.

Perfection

Attention! You own the wire, that's true. But the essential thing is to etch movements in the sky, movements so still they leave no trace. The essential thing is simplicity.

That is why the long path to perfection is horizontal.

Its principles are the following:

If you want the High Wire to transform you into a high-wire walker, you must rediscover the classic purity of this game. But first you must master its technique. Too bad for the one who turns it into a chore.

Above the crowd on your wire you will pass. Pass above and no more. You will be forgotten.

You must not hesitate. Nor should you be conscious of the ground. That is both stupid and dangerous.

The feet are placed in the direction of the wire, the eyes set themselves on the horizon.

The horizon is not a point, it is a continent.

In walking, it is the wire that pushes you. You offer your balancing pole to the wire, perfectly horizontal, arms spread wide apart.

Like a bird, a man perches *on* the wire; he does not lean forward, ready to fall. On the contrary, he must make himself comfortable.

Learn your body: the movement of your arms, the breathing of your fingers, the tension of your toes, the position of your chin, the weight of your elbows. Leave nothing to chance. Chance is a thief that never gets caught.

Eliminate cumbersome exercises. Keep those that transfigure you.

Triumph by seeking out the most subtle difficulties. Reach victory through solitude.

The high-wire walker must rest in the way I have described—and fight in that same way.

Never break the rhythm of a crossing. The cable would start to tremble. For high-wire walking does not mean breathing in unison with the rope, but making sure that this joint breathing does not hinder the breath of the one or the palpitation of the other.

Finally: never fail to attend the performances of high-wire walkers.

Make up your own symbol of perfection. For me, it is throwing away the balancing pole.

With a long and endless gesture, the high-wire walker throws his metal pole far across the sky so that it will not strike the wire, and finds himself alone and helpless, richer and more naked, on a cable made to his own measure. With humility, he now knows he is invincible.

A red velvet wire will be unrolled for him in his dreams. He will move along it brandishing his coat of arms.

In the cities you travel to, always remember to visit the highest monument.

Remain at the top for many hours, looking into the void.

You are a high-wire walker. You cannot go for long without visiting the sky.

Fear

A void like this is terrifying.

Prisoner of a morsel of space, you will struggle desperately against occult elements: the absence of matter, the smell of balance, vertigo from all sides, and the dark desire to return to the ground, even to fall.

This dizziness is the drama of the rope dance, but that is not what I am afraid of.

After long hours of training, the moment comes when there are no more difficulties. Everything is possible, everything becomes easy. It is at this moment that many have perished. But that, no, that is not at all what I am afraid of.

If an exercise resists me during rehearsal, and if it continues to do so a little more each day, to the point of becoming untenable, I prepare a substitute exercise—in case panic grabs me by the throat during a performance. I approach it with more and more reluctance, come to it slyly, surreptitiously. But I always want to persist, to feel the pride of conquering it. In spite of that, I sometimes give up the struggle. But without any fear. I am never afraid on the wire. I am too busy.

But you are afraid of something. I can hear it in your voice. What is it?

Sometimes the sky grows dark around the wire, the wind rises, the cable gets cold, the audience becomes worried. At those moments I hear screams within myself. The wire has stopped breathing. I, too. It is a prelude to catastrophe—like a drumroll announcing the most difficult exercise. In waiting to fall in this way, I have sometimes cursed the wire, but it has never made me afraid.

I know, however, that one day, standing at the edge of the platform, this anguish will appear. One hideous day it will be waiting for me at the foot of the rope ladder. It will be useless for me to shake myself, to joke about it. The next day it will be in my dressing room as I am putting on my costume, and my hands will be wet with horror. Then it will join me in my sleep. I will be crushed a thousand times, rebounding in slow motion in a circus ring, absolutely weightless. When I wake up, it will be stuck to me, indelible, never to leave me again.

And of that, dear heaven, I have a terrible fear.

To imagine that one evening I will have to give up the wire in the same way that so many bullfighters have given up the ring and disappeared into life; that I will have to say, "I was afraid, I met Holy Fear, it invaded me and sucked my blood"—I who hope to give the greatest gift a high-wire walker can give: to die on my wire, leaving to men the insult of a smiling death mask; I who shouted to others on their ropes: "Remember that life is short! What could be better than a happy man in flight, in midair? Think of all the things you've never done!"; I, the fragile walker of wires, the tiniest of men, I will turn away to hide my tears—and yes, how afraid I am.

VARY, FRANCE, WINTER 1972

97

AFTERTHOUGHT

When I was a child, at the dinner table I was often told:

"Behave! Imagine you are at the King's table!"

I, to recapture ardor between my first rehearsals on the wire, always whispered to myself:

"Imagine Fellini is out there hiding, watching you!"

Moments before they are called to the printer, I gather these pages and run away like a thief, to "my cathedral." Past the great brass doors, a refreshing darkness tastes of timelessness. I spiral up the sixty-seven steps to my study, fortress in deep stone. Inside, the lattice of narrow lancets crowning the balcony is coated with a glimmer smoothing the foliage of the capitals. On the old pine board I use as a desk, on the walls, a work in progress stands guard: my pencil drawings of the blocks carved with medieval tools by the cathedral builders in the stoneyard.

Like some predator carrying its take to a higher branch to devour it peacefully, I had to flee the still heat of New York summer to read the book before you do.

I did.

Something is missing.

Not in the text written twelve years ago. Around it.

Away from the core of those ropes and cables, what inhabits my heart today?

A darker shade of gray gradually distorts the contour of each column. The ribs of the vault, above, become barely visible.

An army of clouds must be battling outside. The stained-glass windows are losing their features.

As an adolescent, sleeping on the top of an armoire, I could not understand the rarity of my amorous conquests. A friend suggested I bring the mattress down to the floor and the liaisons proved more numerous. But my sleeping became less felicitous.

Later I decided to dig a tunnel in secret under my parents' country house. My only tools were a teaspoon and my fingernails. I hoped to pass beneath the entire village until I lost the spoon in a cave-in, my nails on the dry earth.

As for the art of magic, I practiced constantly. Being expelled from five different schools made it easier.

I learned to hide, to be on the alert. A street juggler, I broke camp and left no trace.

Then I caught the incurable disease, Excess of Passion: rock climbing, chess, foreign languages, bullfighting, writing, printing, drawing, horseback riding, the theater, motion pictures . . .

I had stolen from the trees the art of Balance. In no time and decidedly alone.

My impatience grew into the desire to avenge myself upon those who slowed me down, who prevented me from writing in the sky, upon the objects which would not bend fast enough under my determination. This is how I learned to juggle—with wrongly turned clubs sold to me by an unscrupulous performer—out of rage and gourmandise.

I kept attacking pyramids. Each time finding the way blocked by a portal called Mediocrity, Jealousy, Intrigue.

Compromise being the key.

I preferred to lockpick them, climb around them, dynamite them.

Not necessarily in that order.

Around my cell, opposing the vehemence of my thoughts, shadows quietly invade every cold vertical line. The glass again becomes luminous. The monument reveals its hundreds of moldings and bosses. The transept receives green, gold, gray, and purple. I witness, like a page being turned, the coming of a new season. The clouds outside have been defeated.

Inside as well.

Why should I think I will never see my wire crossing Niagara Falls?

Or the Sydney Cove?

Never share a stage with Baryshnikov and Menuhin?

And be given a rehearsal hall?

Have my films produced? My plays staged?

Why not rip open the chest of Destiny?

With voracious eyes, staring at the forest of pillars, I am ready to bite the wings of every appeasing thought.

Instead, a sound.

From the crypt. Rising near. Penetrating the grain of the lower slabs. A melody, now. Pouring over the choir, through the transept, along the aisles. And growing. The grand trumpets of the organ are let loose. A prelude. The sun breaks in. The magnificent Gothic vessel is shaken. Fire and clamor consume its sacred geometry.

Echoes . . .

As long as I have a bit of steel rope hanging, I know I'll venture on it. Without the benefit of a single mistake. Like a criminal. In any storm. I have no choice.

To that friend visiting my retreat not long ago, I took the drawing he liked, a boasted ashlar, and wrote "To Werner, for the hell of it!"

Did I mean heaven?

PHILIPPE PETIT

ARTIST-IN-RESIDENCE

THE CATHEDRAL CHURCH

OF ST. JOHN THE DIVINE

NEW YORK CITY, AUGUST 7, 1984

PHILIPPE PETIT,
HIGH-WIRE ARTIST

* = high-wire play: conceived, directed, and
performed by Philippe Petit

1949   Born August 13, in Nemours, France

1966   Discovery of the wire

1967   Character of Le Chat Botté—on the wire—by Jules
Supervielle, direction Isabelle Garma, Maison des
Jeunes et de la Culture, St. Germain-en-Laye, France

1968   Character of the Rope Dancer in *L'if* (with Malika),
Théâtre de l'Amicale, St. Germain-en-Laye, France

1968   Character of Aibric—on the wire—in *Les ombres sur
la mer* (*The Shadowy Waters*), by W. B. Yeats, translation
Antoine Berman, direction Isabelle Garma, Théâtre de
Plaisance, Paris

1971   VALLAURIS, France. Performance for Picasso's 90th
birthday

NOTRE-DAME CATHEDRAL, Paris. Clandestine

1973   SYDNEY HARBOUR BRIDGE, Australia. Clandestine

1974   WORLD TRADE CENTER, New York City. Clandestine

CENTRAL PARK, New York City. Inclined walk over Belvedere Lake

LAON CATHEDRAL, France. Between the two spires, for *Wide World of Sports*

1975   LOUISIANA SUPERDOME, New Orleans. Walk the highest and longest diameter, for the opening of the largest covered stadium in the world

1980   Surprise walk, CATHEDRAL OF SAINT JOHN THE DIVINE, New York City. Inside crossing—Clandestine

1982   CATHEDRAL OF SAINT JOHN THE DIVINE, New York City. Walk celebrating renewal of the cathedral's construction following a 40-year hiatus

Concert in the Sky, Denver. High-wire play for the opening of the World Theater Festival

1983   *Skysong*, New York. High-wire play for the opening of the SUNY Arts Festival

BEAUBOURG/GEORGES POMPIDOU CENTER, Paris. Ascension

1984   *Corde raide et piano volant*, Paris. High-wire play with rock singer Jacques Higelin

PARIS OPÉRA, Paris. High-wire improvisation with opera singer Margarita Zimmermann

MUSEUM OF THE CITY OF NEW YORK, New York City. High-wire performance for the opening of *Daring New York* exhibit

1986   *Ascent*, New York City. Concert for grand piano and high wire on an inclined cable along the nave of the Cathedral of Saint John the Divine

*LINCOLN CENTER, New York City. High-wire performance for the reopening of the Statue of Liberty

1987   *Walking the Harp/A Bridge for Peace*, Jerusalem. High-wire performance on an inclined cable linking the Jewish and Arab quarters for the opening of the Israel Festival under the auspices of Mayor Teddy Kollek

Moondancer, Oregon. High-wire opera for the opening of the Portland Center for the Performing Arts

Grand Central Dances, New York City. High-wire choreography above the concourse of Grand Central Terminal

1988   *From the House of the Dead*, Paris. Creation of the role of the eagle in the Janáček opera (based on the Doestoevsky novel), directed by Volker Schlöndorff

1989   *Tour et fil*, Paris. Spectacular walk—for an audience of 250,000—on an inclined 700-meter cable linking the Palais de Chaillot with the second story of the Eiffel Tower, commemorating the French Bicentennial and the 200th anniversary of the Declaration of the Rights of Man and Citizen, under the auspices of Mayor Jacques Chirac

1990   *American Ouverture*, Paris. High-wire play for the groundbreaking ceremony of the new American Center

1990 *Tokyo Walk*, Japan. Japan's first high-wire perfor-
      mance, to celebrate the opening of the Plaza Mikado
      building in Akasaka

1991 *Viennalewalk*, Austria. High-wire performance
      evoking the history of cinema, for the opening of the
      Vienna International Film Festival under the direction
      of Werner Herzog

1992 *Namur*, Belgium. Inclined walk to the Citadel of Vau-
      ban for a telethon benefiting children with leukemia

      Farinet funambule!, Switzerland. High-wire walk
      portraying the 19th-century "Robin Hood of the Alps,"
      culminated by the harvest of the world's smallest regis-
      tered vineyard to benefit abused children

      The Monk's Secret Longing, New York City. High-wire
      performance for the Regents' Dinner commencing the
      centennial celebrations of the Cathedral of Saint John
      the Divine

1994 *Historischer Hochseillauf*, Germany. Historic high-
      wire walk on an inclined cable from the Paulskirche to
      the Dom, to celebrate the 1,200th anniversary of the
      city of Frankfurt, viewed by 500,000 spectators and the
      subject of a live, nationally broadcast television special

1995 *Catenary Curve*, New York City. Humorous interlude
      during a conference on suspended structures given by
      the architect Santiago Calatrava

1996 *ACT*, New York City. Medieval performance to
      celebrate the 25th anniversary of New York City's most
      innovative youth program

1996   *Crescendo*, New York City. On three different wires set in the nave of the Cathedral of Saint John the Divine, as a farewell tribute to the Very Reverend James Parks Morton, Dean of the Cathedral, and his wife, Pamela

1999   *Millennium Countdown Walk*, New York City. Inauguration of the Rose Center for Earth and Space at the American Museum of Natural History

2002   *Arts on the High Wire*, New York City. Benefit performance for the New York Arts Recovery Fund on an inclined wire at the Hammerstein Ballroom, with clown Bill Irwin and pianist Évelyne Crochet

2002   *Crystal Palace*, New York City. Jacob K. Javits Convention Center

   Crossing Broadway, New York City. Inclined walk, fourteen stories high, for *The Late Show with David Letterman*

2010   *Nikon's Great Performances by Great Artists*: "Above All, Philippe Petit," New York City

2014   *The Song of the Phoenix*, New York City. For the opening of Xu Bing's *Phoenix* at the Cathedral of Saint John the Divine, with saxophonist Paul Winter.

   Look Up! A high-wire apparition to celebrate the 40th anniversary of the WTC walk, at Long House Reserve, East Hampton, New York

2019   *Open Practice*, Brooklyn. SLAM. Combining a typical wire rehearsal with comments and stories.

FILMS

Concert In The Sky (Denver, 1983). Centre Productions, Inc., directed by Mark Elliot

High Wire (New York, 1984). Prairie Dog Productions, directed by Sandy Sissel

Niagara: Miracles, Myths and Magic (Canada, 1986). Philippe plays Blondin. Seventh Man Films for the IMAX System, directed by Kieth Merrill

Tour et fil (France, 1989). FR3/Totem Productions, directed by Alain Hattet

Filmstunde (Austria, 1991). Werner Herzog Productions, directed by Werner Herzog

"Profile of Philippe Petit" (Washington, DC, 1993). *National Geographic Explorer* special

The Man on the Wire (Germany, 1994). Documentary of the rigging and artistic preparations for *Historischer Hochseillauf*. Hessischer Rundfunk Television

Historischer Hochseillauf (Germany, 1994). Live broadcast of the Frankfurt walk. Hessischer Rundfunk Television, directed by Sacha Arnz

Mondo (France, 1995). Costa-Gavras Productions, directed by Tony Gatlif

Secrets of the Lost Empires: "The Incas" (Peru, 1995). PBS/Nova and BBC coproduction, directed by Michael Barnes

Man on Wire (UK, 2008). Academy Award–winning documentary. Wall to Wall / Red Box Films, directed by James Marsh

The Walk (US, 2015). With Joseph Gordon-Levitt playing Philippe. Sony Pictures / Image Movers, IMAX 3D, directed by Robert Zemeckis

THE WIRE WALKER'S
BOOKSHELF

The Ashley Book of Knots by Clifford W. Ashley. New York, Doubleday & Co., 1944.

The Morrow Guide to Knots by Mario Bigon and Guido Regazzoni. New York, Quill, 1982.

Why Knot? by Philippe Petit. New York, Abrams, 2013.

Samson Rope Manual, Boston, MA, Samson Ocean Systems Inc., 1977.

Rigging Manual by D. E. Dickie. Toronto, Ontario, Construction Safety Association of Ontario, 1975.

The Handbook of Rigging by W. E. Rossnagel. New York, McGraw Hill, 1964.

Tensile Structures vol. I and II by Frei Otto. Cambridge, MA, Massachusetts Institute of Technology, 1969.

Architecture du cirque des origines à nos jours by Christian Dupavillon. Paris, Éditions du Moniteur, 1982.

Instant Wind Forecasting by Alan Watts. New York, Dodd, Mead & Company, 1975.

Pocket Weather Forecaster. Woodbury, New York, Barron's, 1974.

Le funambule by Jean Genet. Paris, L'Arbalète, 1958.

Mémoires d'une danseuse de corde: Mme Saqui (1786–1866) by Paul Ginisty. Paris, Librairie Charpentier et Fasquette, 1907.

The Baron in the Trees by Italo Calvino. New York, Harcourt Brace Jovanovich, 1977.

Of Walking in Ice by Werner Herzog. New York, Tanam Press, 1980.

A Book of Five Rings by Miyamoto Musashi. Woodstock, NY, The Overlook Press, 1974.

Master Tree Finder by May T. Watts. Berkeley, CA, Nature Study Guild, 1963.

Nouvelle histoire mondiale de l'aviation by Edmond Petit. Paris, Hachette, 1973.

The Circus of Dr. Lao by Charles G. Finney. New York, Vintage/Random House, 1983.

Le petit cirque by Fred. Paris, Dargaud, 1973.

Traité de podologie by Docteur Boris J. Dolto. Paris, Maloine, 1982.

Tao of Jeet Kune Do by Bruce Lee. Burbank, CA, Ohara Publications Inc., 1975.

La barre-fixe by Paul Masino and Georges Chautemps. Paris, Vigot Frères, 1961.

Neige et roc by Gaston Rebuffat. Paris, Hachette, 1959.

Paroles sur le mime by Étienne Decroux. Paris, NRF/Galli-
mard, 1963.

The Theater and Its Double by Antonin Artaud. New York,
Grove Press Inc., 1958.

Leonardo on the Human Body by Leonardo da Vinci. New York,
Dover Publications, 1983.

La merveilleuse histoire du cirque by Henry Thétard. Paris, Jul-
liard, 1978.

Tsirk by Shuier & Slavsky. Moscow, Izdatielsvo Covietskaia
Encyclopedia, 1973.

Circus History by Iwao Akuna. Tokyo, Nishida Shoten, 1977.

Le grand livre du cirque vol. I and II by Monica J. Renevey.
Genève, Edito-Service S. A., 1977.

Histoire et légende du cirque by Roland Auguet. Paris, Flam-
marion, 1974